Mail Order
The Widow's Choice

By
Faith Johnson

Clean and Wholesome Western
Historical Romance

Copyright © 2023 by Faith Johnson

All rights reserved.
No part of this book may be
reproduced, stored in a retrieval
system, or transmitted in any form, or
by any means, electronic, mechanical,
photocopying, recording or otherwise,
without prior permission of the author
or publisher.

Printed in the United States of America

Table of Contents

Unsolicited Testimonials

By **Glaidene Ramsey**
★★★★★ I so enjoy reading Faith Johnson's stories. This Bride and groom met as she arrived in town. They were married and then the story begins.!!!! Enjoy

By **Voracious Reader**
★★★★★ "Great story of love and of faith. The hardships we may have to go through and how with faith, and God's help we can get through them" -

By **Glaidene's reads**
★★★★★ "Faith Johnson is a five star writer. I have read a majority of her books. I enjoyed the story and hope you will too!!!!!"

By **Kirk Statler**
★★★★★ I liked the book. A different twist because she wasn't in contract with anyone when she went. She went. God provided for her needs. God blessed her above and beyond.

By **Amazon Customer**
★★★★★ Great clean and easy reading, a lot of fun for you to know ignores words this is crazy so I'll not reviewing again. Let me tell it and go

By **Kindle Customer**
★★★★★ Wonderful story. You have such a way of showing people that opposite do attack. Both in words and action. I am glad that I found your books.

Just to say thanks for checking our works we like to gift you

Our Exclusive Never Before Released Books

100% FREE!

Please GO TO

http://cleanromancepublishing.com/gift

And get your FREE gift

Thanks for being such a wonderful client.

PROLOGUE

Nevada, 1865

Simon Perry sat at his old oak desk in the dusty back office of Perry Grocery Store with a small half-empty bottle of whiskey and a glass. He felt light-headed, and the room slowly began to whirl around him.

There was a knock on the door, and he barely managed a "Come in." It was Harry Smith, his long-time friend who owned the barbershop next door.

"You okay, Simon?" Harry's voice held concern, and he entered the office and noticed the whiskey. "Should you be drinking that?"

Simon felt his head loll to one side as he slurred, "Yeah, I'm good. How good could a man be?" He hiccupped. "What good is a man who returns home to an empty house?"

"I'm sorry," Harry replied sympathetically. He hunched down and stared into his friend's glassy eyes. "Laurie came by as often as she could to help clean up, and John managed the store for you."

Simon belched and his eyes fluttered. "You have a wonderful wife and son… I do not. What good is a man with an empty home and without a wife to welcome him home from fighting for his country?"

"It's not your fault, Simon," Harry said, raising a brow at his friend. "This is not you. Is this how you want to spend your first few days home? Go on to bed." He stood to his feet, wrapped his arms around Simon's thick arm, and tried to pull him up with a heave at the dead weight.

"No. No, I can do… myself. It's only a small whiskey, and I will finish it." Simon ignored Harry's attempts to help him up from the chair. He was in pain and wanted to drain it away, and what better way than whiskey?

"Fine." Harry sighed, stood to his full height, and looked at him with a concerned frown. "If you need anything, we're right next door. You're not alone…"

"I am… I am… alone." Simon lifted his glass, took a gulp, and poured in more liquid. "Go be with your family… leave me be. I'll be fine. Please, leave me be."

"Alright." Harry tapped his friend on his shoulder. "I'll check on you later."

Simon drained his glass, listening to Harry's steady footsteps on the hardwood, followed by the *ting* of the door as it closed behind him.

He drew in a deep breath and felt his heart torn apart in the same way his mind thought about those buildings that had crumbled at every cannon blast.

His eyes darted to the letter that sprawled across his desk, and he swallowed down tears that formed behind his eyes. Its words echoed in his mind, and he loathed himself for taking another swig of whiskey.

Dear Simon

My love, please forgive me. The days drag on, I am lonely every night, and every day I am alone. I miss you, but I have been quite patient. Three years have been long, and I can wait no longer.

I must bid you farewell as I have met a charming man who can take me away and live a good life. Guilt fills me as I do not know if you will ever read this letter or if you will come home.

If you return, I pray you will find love just as I have found love.

Sincerely,
Harriet

And that was the last he had heard from his wife.

Simon felt the warm sensation of gentle waves rocking the sides of a boat in a calm river waiting for fish to bite. It was soothing and peaceful. His eyes drooped, and the bottle of whiskey looked hazy. He reached out his hand for the bottle, but his eyes closed, and he fell facedown on the table, knocking the bottle with a slight thud.

Warm liquid saturated his hand, and everything went black.

CHAPTER ONE

Pennsylvania, 1868, three years later

Catherine Myers scurried along the highly polished maple floor and down the long narrow passageway. She was careful to keep her head down as she passed the staircase holding freshly pressed, bleached white linen from the laundry room.

She took a quick side glance through the ornately designed cast iron wrought banister and breathed a sigh of relief. The last thing she wanted was for the housekeeper to find her taking the stairs at the front of the house.

The servant stairs had to be blocked off for cleaning, as the master of the house had discarded a trolley full of last night's meal down the stairs in a drunken rage. At a moment's whim, he had changed his mind from roasted beef to roasted duck, and getting duck was near to impossible.

She found Joan waiting patiently for the linen in the main bedroom, her fingers interlocked within her clasped hands. A pretty young maid dressed neatly in her well-fitted navy and white uniform, she had unfortunately caught the master's eye.

Catherine gave a slight shake of her head with a *tut*. The poor girl was at the master's beck and call.

"Here you go, sorry for the wait," Catherine handed over the linen with a slight pant. "Don't tell Mrs. Canning that I took the front stairs entrance. You know what the master did last night."

Joan's face was pale, and she nodded with a small, forced smile. "Thank you. He was in a foul mood this morning, and he should be back from hunting soon and will want to retire."

"I understand." She placed a hand on Joan's shoulder with a comforting squeeze. "You should not be here. A young girl like you…" She paused with a sigh as she thought of her daughter. "You should be married at the side of a gentleman."

Joan giggled, and color returned to her cheeks. "There are few of those around." She placed the linen on the bed and began to make up the bed. "I may leave soon, though," she added, causing Catherine to stop at the door. She looked at Joan in surprise. "But, please, don't tell anyone."

"What do you mean?" Catherine's brows knitted. "You're thinking of going back home?"

Joan shook her head vehemently. "No, I will never return home. As much as the master is always in a foul mood and the mistress is jealous, it is better here than with my father."

"So, where are you going?" Catherine knew time was of the essence, and she had to start cleaning the parlor, but curiosity got the best of her.

Her voice dropped to barely a whisper. "I found one of the master's newspapers, and there is a page for mail order brides."

Catherine's mouth fell agape. "For what? You're joking?"

"I've written letters to a man in Ohio, Josh Owens, who needs a wife to help him at his ranch."

"In the west?" Catherine stared at the girl wide-eyed. Joan's face was serious. She returned Catherine's gaze, and her eyes filled with fear.

"You won't tell anyone, would you?" Joan begged. She stopped flapping the sheets over the mattress, and her face flushed. "The master would be angry." She paused. "Josh sent me a photograph and… I haven't seen anyone so fine-looking before."

"Of course, I won't say a thing." Catherine smiled with a slight shake of her head. "Not even to my children."

"Michelle will be sad, won't she?" Joan said with a hint of sadness herself as she resumed making the bed. "I've made some real friends here, and I will miss them, especially Michelle."

"She will understand," Catherine replied without confidence. Her daughter tended to hold strong affections toward her friends. "Besides, I think she will be too busy running after Miss Jane."

"I won't miss that spoiled brat." Joan's face pinched, and Catherine chuckled. "She is quite nasty, isn't she?"

"Well, we all know how it is." Catherine tucked back a few strands that escaped her cap. "Money can buy anything except for good manners. Anyway, I should go. If Mrs. Canning finds me elsewhere, I'll have a beating, and I'm getting too old for that."

"I wouldn't say thirty-four is old," Joan responded with a fresh smile, and she seemed relieved. "You should have a look in the newspaper, too."

"What? No." Catherine felt horrified. "Michelle is far too young to even think about marriage. She is only fourteen."

"I mean, for you." Joan pursed her lips. "Just think about it. I saw many advertisements for older folk, men, and women, but you're not old."

What a ridiculous notion, Catherine thought, amused. "I'll think about it. Thank you, Joan. Good luck for when the master returns."

"I'll need it," Catherine heard Joan reply as she left and headed toward the parlor using the same entrance as before.

***

"This can't be true," Michelle whispered. Her hands covered her tear-stained face as she sat on the edge of the bed. "Why didn't she say anything?"

"I'm sorry, love." Catherine pulled her daughter into a tight hug. "Joan wanted to say goodbye, but you know she couldn't say anything. Just look at how angry the master is now. He is finding fault with everything. I even feel sorry for Mrs. Canning."

"She told you. Why couldn't she tell me?" Michelle's face was downcast. She struggled from her mother's tight grip, and Catherine let go.

"I just happened to be there." Catherine shrugged and felt her heart clench at the pain on her daughter's face. "I think she just wanted to tell someone and I was around."

"Stephen is also upset." Michelle's voice was full of disdain, and Catherine sighed. She wondered if Joan had thought of the consequences of her departure for those left in Lindsay Manor. No one could blame her. It was her chance at happiness and a free life. Between Michelle and Stephen, her eleven-year-old son who worked in the stables, she could not toss a coin to decide who suffered most.

Since Joan's departure, Stephen and the other stable boys had to scrub the stalls late every night. For everyone, work had doubled, and only the mistress walked nonchalantly around the manor with a great smile and a bottle of wine over dinner every night.

Miss Jane and the young Master Timothy had gone to New York to spend time with their aunt and uncle.

"You should be relieved," Catherine soothed. Her mouth curved to one side, and lines creased the corners of her eyes. "Now that Miss Jane will be away for a few weeks, you can keep busy in the scullery. Not like your brother who has the master at his heels."

"I miss her, Mom. She was my first friend." Michelle buried her head into her hands and sobbed.

Catherine placed her arm around her daughter and whispered, "I know, love. I know."

Sharp, quick footsteps grew louder, and Catherine closed her eyes. Taking a deep breath, she waited.

"What's going on?" a deep female voice resonated through the servants' quarters. From Catherine's view of the room, she could see Mrs. Canning standing like a sea captain, hands on her hips, her face full of fury. "Where is everyone? The master demands the parlor be cleaned. He isn't happy." She paused for a breath, and her eyes roamed until she finally made eye contact. "Catherine, it's your responsibility. Go before the master beats you himself."

"Stay strong, love." Catherine squeezed her daughter. "I'll see you later. If you see your brother, tell him I'll find a way out of this…"

"How?" Michelle replied bitterly. "Are you going to get married, too?"

Catherine was taken aback by her daughter's outburst. "Michelle, I—"

"I said, go!" Mrs. Canning boomed, her eyes never leaving Catherine. "Or should I tell the master you'd prefer to sleep on the streets?"

Her steely blue eyes were cold and wisps from her light blond hair framed her face. Catherine decided at one time that Mrs. Canning might have been beautiful. "Tell your daughter not to slack off now that Miss Jane is away."

Catherine sighed, gave a small nod, and tapped her daughter's shoulder as she stood to her feet. "Run along to the scullery before Mrs. Canning has a go at you, too."

"Yes. Mom… I'm sorry for what I said," she heard Michelle say while walking out of the room.

Catherine ignored the sharp gaze of Mrs. Canning. Chin lifted in the air, she headed toward the parlor where she found two other maids cleaning an already spotless room.

"Pick up the cloth over there." One of the maids, Jessie, pointed to a few cloths in the corner of the room. "The master wasn't happy with the windows."

Catherine looked between Jessie, just as young as Joan was, and the tall rectangular windows. The glass was as clear as the crystal she had polished in the morning. She glimpsed through the windows at the light brown trees reflecting colors of gold and auburn into the parlor. Nevertheless, she found a clean cloth and a bucket filled with water and began to clean the first of ten tall windows.

"What do you think about this mail order bride?" Jessie asked one of the other maids, carefully dusting the brass light fixtures. Catherine did not recognize her and wondered if she was new. Maybe a quick replacement for Joan?

"It's daring," she replied casually, clearly uninterested. "I can't say I would do it."

"What if Joan really does find love?" Jessie inquired. She began wiping the oak tables to a shine that gave the sun competition.

"In the west, of all places," the maid responded with the same carefree tone. "There is nothing in the west, I'm sure of it. Let alone love."

"I can't help but think," Jessie hesitated and dropped her tone to a whisper, "what if Joan is right? Maybe there is another life out there."

Catherine rolled her eyes and listened as the two debated about mail order brides, the west, and love. If only life were that simple. She had had her chance at love, and she knew it would never happen again. Marriage was for the young girls, not for widows like her, especially with two children.

Time seemed to drag as she reached the fourth window and tried to shield her eyes from the glare of the sun as it slowly moved toward the west.

Catherine heaved as she reached up to wipe the top and felt an object to her side, followed by a clank. Her heart pounded. Only the most expensive decorated vases were placed in the parlor. Nervously, she looked down and noticed the pool of water that gathered on the mantel from the vase she'd knocked over.

"It's alright." Catherine noticed the concern and fearful eyes in her direction, and she assured Jessie and the other maid no harm was done. "Just a vase with a bit of water. I'll clean it up."

Catherine bent over and found a newspaper stuck between the table and the wall. It probably had been missed by the master and fell behind the table. She thought over what Joan had said about the matrimony advertisements between women and men her age.

She glanced at the maids from the corner of her eye, noticing all were absorbed in their chatter and cleaning duties, and opened the newspaper to the matrimonial section. Her eyes widened at two full pages of advertisements.

Maybe there was something out there and perhaps a chance for a better life for Michelle and Stephen. She felt her eyes sting at the memories of their past life when her husband was alive and how happy they had all been. Malcolm had been the love of her life, a good father, and she missed him more than life itself.

Catherine perused the advertisements. Joan's words flowed through her mind, and one small ad caught her eye. She did not know quite why she took an interest or why she tore out the page and pocketed it. All she thought about was Michelle and Stephen.

She quickly cleaned up the mess, and for the first time in years, she felt hopeful. Her heart leaped at the thought of responding to Mr. Simon Perry's request for a woman of good habits and housekeeping experience, aged between thirty and thirty-five years.

CHAPTER TWO

Nevada, 1868, one month later

The door opened with a soft ring as Simon entered Smith's Barbershop. Dark walnut tables were neatly pushed against the wall, each with wooden Koken barber chairs facing small Victorian oval-shaped mirrors mounted on the wall.

Not many people were around at this time of morning, and he thought he would get a head start on the day. He breathed in the fresh smell of shaving cream.

Harry looked surprised as he entered the room from the door between the shop and his home.

"You're early," he remarked humorously. "In fact, I wasn't expecting you at all." A curious grin spread across his robust features.

Simon chuckled as he sat comfortably on one of the chairs and rested his feet on the steel footrest.

"I decided it was high time I got a clean shave and a haircut." Simon peered at his reflection in the mirror before him. He raked his hand through his light brown hair, but his fingers caught in tangled knots.

"I'd say," Harry agreed, covering Simon's chest with a thick sheet. He began to sharpen the blades of his shaving knives on a thick leather strap. "So, today's the big day, huh?"

"Yup," Simon responded, pursing his lips as Harry began to apply shaving cream. "The train will arrive at ten forty."

"I haven't seen you this excited since the time Laurie brought over carrot cake for your birthday when you came back home." Harry moved the blade across Simon's cheeks in quick swift motions.

"Mmm," Simon replied and closed his eyes. His heart pounded at the feel of cold, sharp steel against his skin. Within a few minutes, Simon drew in a deep breath and exhaled slowly, relieved the shave was over. "Yes, I think it was a good idea. Her daughter can help at the grocery store, and her son can help me at the farm. John won't mind, would he?"

Harry was silent for a moment as he put away the shaving equipment and readied the instruments for the haircut. John was his eldest son and, at twenty years of age, managed the grocery store for Simon.

"I don't see why not," Harry said casually. He tilted his head to look down at Simon and added, with a raised brow, "You're the boss, and some company will do him good. What's her name again?"

"Catherine. A real pretty name, don't you think?" Simon returned his friend's gaze, and a corner of his mouth tipped upward.

Harry nodded, looked over Simon's hair, and whistled through his teeth. "I don't remember ever cutting your hair. I'm no priest, can't perform miracles, but I'll try to make you decent for your bride."

Simon bellowed with laughter. "Thank you. Much obliged."

***

Simon shifted from one foot to the other. He looked at the small dusty clock mounted above the entrance of the train station. His hands felt clammy and his shoulders tense. For the first time since he sent Catherine the invitation to come to Nevada, he wondered if this was a mistake. His life would change. He was not only taking on a new wife but also two children. She wrote a lot about them and was clearly proud.

He placed a balled hand to his mouth and coughed. It was almost eleven, and the train had not arrived yet. He was tired of the air thick from ash and soot, but saved by the cool wind.

Brown, crisp leaves were scattered amongst the feverish-yellow and pale green grass. He glimpsed at the sky, slowly gathering soft puffy gray clouds, and breathed a soft sigh. He knew it would rain later, and the fields would become mush.

A loud scrape of metal on metal interrupted his thoughts as whistling and tooting burst through the air like a stampede of cattle. He felt the hot rush of air as the train rattled past him. The wheels screeched forcibly to a final halt, followed by a hiss as steam formed dark puffs of smoke in its wake.

Simon straightened his broad shoulders to hide the apprehension that filled him the closer he walked toward the train. Although he had managed to purchase first-class tickets for Catherine and her children, they did not have the privilege of a private carriage. Still, she had assured him it would be fine.

Shielding his eyes with his hand from the filtering light through the clouds, his eyes darted between the crowds of people that blocked his view. He never understood the sense of feathery hats, large bustle skirts and ornate dresses, top silk hats, and uncomfortable black suits. He nodded at the few who pushed past him wearing clothes that were more practical.

"Simon Perry?" A warm, cultured voice caught his attention, and he turned to face the entrance. Sandwiched between groups of people, Catherine stood valiant and beautiful beside her children. Their attention was focused on the depot full of activity.

"Yes," Simon nodded. He realized he held his breath and exhaled slowly. She was dressed in a modest emerald-green dress that flattered her curvy figure with puffed sleeves narrowing to her wrist. Her dark walnut eyes captivated him, as did her dark brown hair tinted red like a robin in flight bathed in sunlight.

Her features were soft with high cheekbones and her skin smooth. Her daughter had similar features and hair color except for her eyes, a cool blue like her brother. Stephen was tall for a boy his age, had a strong jaw, and appeared fit. He peered at Simon through unruly blond hair that fell across his face.

"Catherine," Simon said as he regained his composure, realizing he had been staring at her and noticed her whisper something to her children.

"Hello, Mr. Perry," they said, simultaneously looking at him.

"I'm glad you got here." He felt like a child as embarrassment overtook him. "I see you have quite a few suitcases. Let me bring the wagon closer. It will be easier to load—"

"No, it's alright. We've carried much heavier items." Catherine nodded toward Stephen, who let out a deep, frustrated sigh.

"I insist. You've been on a long journey and must be tired." Simon noticed the relief on both Michelle and Stephen's faces and the creases on Catherine's face. "I'll bring the wagon around. It's not a problem."

His pulse raced at the sight of her dazzling smile, a mix of happiness and appreciation. He quickly turned away and headed toward the wagon. He felt sweaty and flushed, and enjoyed the rush of cool wind against his skin.

After heaving some of the luggage, he was thankful to have brought the wagon closer. Some of the suitcases were ridiculously heavy and felt like bags of wheat.

"I'd like to stop at my grocery store before we head out to the farm. I forgot to get some supplies this morning." Simon glanced at Catherine sitting next to him. She smelled of flowers in spring, and he felt the heat of her body.

She seemed surprised. "Yes, I don't mind."

"You see, my farm does supply the grocery store, but there are items I don't provide," Simon explained. He failed to mention he had promised Harry to stop off at the grocery store for him, Laurie, and John to meet them. "It's a small town and will only take a couple of minutes."

The few minutes lasted about an hour, and Simon remembered why he had wanted to delay Laurie Smith, Harry's cheery wife, from meeting Catherine.

"It's lovely to meet you. I work at the bakery a few blocks away, and you must come over some time," Laurie gushed with excitement and pulled an unwilling Stephen and Michelle into a hug. Her plump arms gave them a tight squeeze. "I'd love to have you all try some of our baked goods. And these youn' ones will love our tarts, sweets, carrot cake, and apple pie.

"We live just next door to the grocery. Harry is the best barber in Carson."

"I appreciate your kind offer." Catherine gave a friendly smile. The grocery store's door was left open for John to load the wagon. Simon heard footsteps on the hardwood floor, and they stopped. He turned around and found John standing like a shoulder in the middle of the shop. Simon raised a brow with a rib-tickling grin at the young man's beet-red cheeks as he stared at Michelle.

Simon stepped forward, thinking he would help John from his awkward situation. "You packed it all already?"

John was much like Harry, with chiseled features and blue-green eyes, but he had his mother's fair hair and complexion.

"Yes, sir," John stammered and turned his attention to Simon. He began to read out the small list Simon had given him.

"Thanks, that'll be all. We best get going then." Simon stretched his arms high into the air and added, "The farm's about two hours away from here, near Carson Valley."

Half an hour later, they were en route to the farm.

"I expect the kids will want to go to school?" Simon glanced at Catherine, who returned a smile and bobbed her head.

"They would, yes," she covered her mouth as she yawned, "Excuse me," she blushed.

Simon chuckled, "Nothing to excuse. You've traveled long. You can get some sleep if you like."

Not a minute later, he saw her head roll to one side. She had fallen fast asleep.

CHAPTER THREE

Two weeks had gone by. The marriage had been delayed since the pastor was out of town, but he was due to return soon.

To Catherine's great pleasure, Simon had enrolled Michelle and Stephen in school the day after they arrived at the farm. It was late in the afternoon, and Catherine expected them to return soon with large appetites. She wandered around the quiet farmhouse. It had been quick to clean, unlike the Lindsay Manor, where it took one day just to clean one room.

She thought over her first meeting with Simon. His masculine features made her feel butterflies in her stomach, and she could barely hide her emotions. Even now, she felt a strange sensation toward him that she did not recognize or maybe had forgotten. She reminded herself this was to be a marriage of convenience and a chance for them to have a happy life. But she was not to expect love. Not at her age.

She knew Michelle and Stephen had felt uncomfortable at first, but not anymore. Stephen and Michelle enjoyed their own rooms with beautiful views on the second floor, each with simple oak beds, a cupboard, a desk with drawers, and a chair to match.

Her room was more than she could have imagined. It was similar to her children's, except it was a bit larger with a double bed and a wonderful view of Carson Valley along the horizon.

She headed to the kitchen and rubbed her arms as a shiver ran down her spine. She lit the brick stove, adding a few more logs of wood.

Hard thumping sounded from the front porch, and the door burst open, followed by excited chatter.

"No, Stephen, it doesn't go like that," Michelle insisted, her steps just as loud as her brother's.

"Yes, it does. Just look, I will show you. You're not making it properly."

Their footsteps stopped in the dining room, and Catherine grinned as she heard the shuffling and crinkling of papers.

She walked to the dining room and found them huddled around the oak dining table, folding pieces of newspaper.

"What are you doing?" Catherine watched Stephen carefully fold a torn square-shaped piece into a triangle and turn it over. Michelle's eyes were fixated, and Catherine enforced with a stern tone. "Hello? What are you doing?"

"Oh, hi, Mom." Michelle turned her head, gave a quick sweet smile, and returned her attention to her brother.

"I'm busy, Mom." Stephen stuck his tongue out the corner of his lips, and his brows knitted from avid concentration.

Catherine heard heavy footsteps approach from behind and flinched. She had planned to have lunch outside on the back porch but got caught up in her children's unusual task.

"Why's everyone congregating in here? Is there someth—" Simon paused and raised his brow at Stephen with amusement as a broad smile scrawled across his face. He walked closer to the table. "Hey now, you got it, but let me show you how to make it better."

Simon grabbed a large piece of newspaper, folded it and tore it in half, and began folding a neat little boat in expert fashion.

"Ah, I want to do that." Stephen stared at him with admiration. "The kids at school won't believe it."

"Please, teach me too," Michelle begged with a hopeful look. "Tomorrow, everyone will go to the lake and sail their boats."

Simon guffawed and gave Catherine a proud look. "Of course, I was a champion in my day." His face lit up like a little boy who had received his first wooden toy. "After lunch, I'll take you to the lake and show you how to get it to float. It's a real skill, and then your friends will be amazed when it sails like one of those ships out at sea for months."

"Really?" Stephen beamed and turned to his mom. "Please, please, can we go?"

"We'll do chores and homework when we get back, promise," Michelle pleaded.

Catherine gazed at Simon, who returned her stare with crinkled eyes and a curved smile. She felt goosebumps run over her skin. She could not help but feel bothered, but at the same time, she was happy he and her children were bonding.

"Oh, alright." Catherine lifted her hands in resignation and rolled her eyes playfully while Michelle and Stephen yelled with excitement. "I'll do your chores, and when you get back, you finish your homework."

Simon stood to his feet. The expression on his face had not changed. "On my way here, I could not stop thinking about food. I'm starved." He turned to Michelle and Stephen. "Do you think we could have some lunch now?"

Both Michelle and Stephen's heads bobbed with enthusiasm plastered on their faces.

Catherine had learned Simon liked fruit, and she had gathered a fine bowl of berries. The table was also laden with biscuits, chicken, and potatoes.

She smiled, watching Stephen and Michelle gobble their lunch as fast as they could and glance at Simon, who purposefully took his time playing with his food.

He humorously glimpsed at them out the corner of his eye, pretending not to notice their eager stares, and reached out for a glass of water. Both Michelle and Stephen exchanged hopeful glances and remained silent.

"Okay." Simon suddenly pushed his chair back, reached out for another buttered biscuit, and said with a wink, "Let's go make and sail some boats."

**

Catherine kept looking out the windows. She paced the front porch as the sky began to lose its dull blue to dusty red, fearing that something had happened to Simon, Michelle, and Stephen. *Surely, they should be back by now,* she thought and wondered whether to send one of the hired farmworkers to Harry and send out a search party.

She stood in the kitchen, biting her nails, and looked over the meal she had prepared. She could not find most of her ingredients, so she had to settle for soup and cornbread, but she was confused why there was so little in the pantry, for she was certain they had received new supplies.

The sounds of horse hooves and the crunching and slushing from wagon wheels interrupted her thoughts. She ran out to the porch, relieved to see them and that they were in good spirits.

"What took you so long?" Catherine inquired as Michelle and Stephen climbed off the wagon, its canvas top lowered. "I was getting worried." Her eyes darted between the two, and her eyes widened. "You're both soaked. Get inside and dry yourselves, or you'll get sick."

"Oh, Mom…" Stephen whined and pushed his shoulders back, lifting his chin.

"Listen to your mother," Simon told him gently with an expression of mirth. "We have quite the story to tell, don't we?"

Michelle and Stephen burst into laughter and ran inside the house.

"What was that about?" Catherine turned to face Simon, who remained in the driver's seat. "Have they gone mad?"

He chuckled and looked pleased. "I'll be back in a minute or two after I've parked the wagon."

Catherine did not respond. She watched him tug at the reins, and the horse trotted toward the carriage shed, pulling the wagon along. She hesitated, wanting to say something, but instead, she went inside to question Michelle and Stephen as her curiosity grew.

Their voices carried throughout the farmhouse, which had been unthought of at the Lindsay Manor. She was thrilled they could grow up happy. In the beginning, she had been nervous. But now she knew she had made the right decision coming to the west, and in the short time they had been with Simon Perry, she did not want anything to change. The thought of him made her smile, and she had to admit she felt jittery at times and stole looks at him whenever she saw he was busy.

It was the same every night at the dinner table; she could not help but appreciate his smile and hung onto his every word as he told stories about the farm. Sometimes she thought he caught on to her silent looks, but he never said anything.

"I'm sorry." Catherine felt her cheeks flush at the stares from her children and Simon, who were seated around the dining room table. She brought the pot of soup to the table. "I could only make soup and cornbread. I... I could have sworn that the pantry was full. I'm sure it was full this afternoon, and..." She stopped talking when she heard snickering from the table and frowned, noticing Simon was the instigator.

"It's alright, Mom," Stephen chuckled, "It was Mr. Perry's idea. We went along with it."

"I don't know what you mean." Simon feigned innocence, palms up in the air, but his expression was one of guilt.

"Please, someone, tell me what's going on?" Catherine insisted, and her feeling of embarrassment quickly transformed into annoyance.

"There is food, Mom." Michelle had an equally guilty look on her sweet face. "While you were busy cleaning up…"

"Before we left for the lake," Stephen interrupted and received a glare from his sister.

"We snuck back inside," Michelle's voice rose above her brother's, "and took out items from the pantry…" She started to giggle, as did Stephen and Simon. "We hid them. The groceries are safe, in the shed. Sorry, Mom."

"It was not our idea, promise." Stephen stopped and pressed his lips together.

Catherine stared at them, and for a moment, they stopped laughing. She bit her lip and inhaled deeply. They had played a joke on her. Or rather, Simon had.

"Hey, stop ratting me out." Simon leaned toward Stephen and gave him a friendly nudge. "I thought we were in this together."

Catherine could not help but smile at the scene unfolding before her. "I don't suppose the same thing happened last week when I was to make a meat pie. I couldn't find any meat until after I made apple pie?"

Small bouts of laughter came from the table. Simon replied, "Yes, guilty as charged. I took Stephen with me to the field, and we decided on apple pie. We overheard you share your dinner plans with Michelle…

and with her help…" He paused, trying to stifle a laugh. "It was a good idea, wasn't it? The apple pie, I mean."

Catherine sat down at the table and shared their good spirits as they confessed to other comical mysteries and crimes that had happened over the past week. While she had been doing laundry, the soap disappeared, including the spares, and she had to stop washing the sheets. Later in the day, she found all the soap in her room on her desk of drawers.

"If you could halt your pranks for a while, I'd be very grateful." Catherine gave a slight shake of her head in amusement and turned to Simon. "You're more of a child than Stephen."

"I confess, it's true." Simon's eyes crinkled, and she felt a small tug in her chest at the bliss on his face. "Though let me tell you, he and Michelle will have no problems sailing their boats in the river tomorrow."

"We're experts now, Mom." Stephen beamed and dipped his bread in the soup.

"Until you pushed me into the lake," Michelle accused with an exasperated look. "My boat sank to the bottom. It didn't come up."

"Then Mr. Perry pushed me," Stephen added. "But we got him good."

"So that's how you both got wet." Catherine poured coffee into her cup. "How did you get away in staying dry?" she prodded Simon, who leaned back in his chair and gazed at her earnestly.

"I'm not dry at all. They found weeds and the like, got them wet, and threw them at me." Simon tried to act horrified, but the humor in his eyes gave him away.

"I think you had more fun than my children," Catherine responded with a wide smile. She felt warmth rise within her chest at the sound as he roared with laughter.

"If you could've seen it." Simon shook his head, slowly regaining composure, and reached for coffee. "Next time, you should join us."

"Only to be pushed into the lake?" Catherine returned his mischievous smile. "I don't think so."

Their eyes locked from across the table, and she felt the breath knocked from her chest. She knew her children were talking but did not know what they were saying. His captivating eyes stopped her world. Her lips parted as she took in a deep breath and breathed out slowly as she looked down at her bowl of soup.

Why did he have this effect on her? Why did her heart beat faster?

She remembered once, years ago, when she had experienced a similar cozy warm-hearted feeling, but this could not be right. A person would only find one love in their life. She could not have feelings for a man other than her deceased husband. She pushed her thoughts aside, focused on her meal, and listened to Michelle and Stephen chatter about school.

CHAPTER FOUR

Simon felt refreshed and stood in the field, watching his workers plow the soil deeply. His eyes followed the distant rolling hills, covered in yellow and pale-green grass. He saw cattle from neighboring farms dotted on the flat plains peacefully grazing.

His mind drifted to the day he moved to the farm and how excited but nervous he felt at becoming a farmer. It was the same feeling he had now when he was near Catherine. She was not just a pretty face. She was smart. He liked her kindness, and how she interacted with her children made him feel a pull in his heart.

Sometimes, the way she looked at him made him want to take her into his arms and never let go.

A rush of wind filled his ears, and he thought he could hear her warm voice. He heard someone calling his name and was taken aback to find Catherine approaching him.

"Oh, I hope you're not upset." Catherine appeared flustered and red-faced as she handed him a small basket. "I meant to give this to you before you left this morning."

He took the basket and peered inside. "Thanks, but you didn't need to go through all this trouble." She had come out all this way just to give him a basket full of snacks, and he suddenly felt shy. "What I mean to say is… you didn't need to go through all that trouble just for me."

He felt powerless under her gaze, and the intense look on her face made his knees weak.

"I had to," Catherine insisted. "Over the last few days, you haven't made it to lunch. I know you're busy, but it is important to eat, you know." She stood to one side, hands on her hips and her head tilted as if searching for something.

"Yes, you're right. I'm sorry." Simon's head bobbed quickly. "By the time I get back home, I'm famished. So I think this lunch basket is a good idea. I see you packed salted beef and apples here..." He gave a boyish grin. "Thank you."

"You're welcome," Catherine responded and relaxed her arms, clasping her hands together, fingers entwined. "I wanted to also thank you for being good to Stephen and Michelle."

His mouth twitched into a half-smile, and he shifted his weight to one leg as he propped the basket on his hip. "It's alright, I don't mind. They're good kids."

"Yes, they are." Catherine agreed with a proud smile, and her cheeks looked rosy. "I don't think I ever asked why you never had children of your own." She paused. "Not that it's any of my business. There's no need to answer...I—"

Simon gave a loud chuckle. "C'mon, let's go for a walk." He jerked his head toward the valley. "My men have everything sorted from here on; they don't need me to watch their every move."

Catherine fell in step next to him. He was thrilled she had come out to the field, even if it was just to bring him lunch. Maybe he would find other excuses to get her to visit him in the future. What if he left his lunch basket behind on purpose? Would she bring it to him or let someone else do it?

"I've always liked children," Simon said as he held the basket firm in his hand. "Soon after I took complete control over the grocery store, my father passed away. He didn't tell anyone that he had been sick."

"I'm sorry," she said. He heard the sincere heartfelt sadness in her voice, "I was close to my father, and when he passed away, I felt my world had crumbled. He got to see his grandchildren, but they don't have much memory of him."

"Yes, it's not easy." Simon stole a glance at her and saw her brave smile. In that brief moment of shared sadness, he thought she was a miracle. "Then, I had to join the war and leave home." A shadow fell over his face. "But anyway, I like children. I have always wanted some of my own."

Catherine gave a small nod. "I think you make a fine father."

"That's kind of you to say." He smiled, pleased.

"It's true." Catherine stopped in her tracks, and the earnest look in her eyes made his heart quicken. "Stephen and Michelle speak little else about anything since the trip to the lake, Not to mention their continuous confessions of every prank they did and insist were all your ideas."

"Really. now?" Simon bit his lip to suppress his smile and felt his heart jump. "Then perhaps I'd best lie low for a while until the heat is gone and forgotten." He paused for a moment and watched her break into laughter. He felt he could watch her all day.

"You admit it." Catherine gave him a mischievous look. "You finally admit it."

"Alright, yes, I humbly confess." He looked at her, pleased he could make her happy, and wondered what she was thinking. "I was wondering, and if I may ask, what happened to their father?"

The smile on her face quickly disappeared, and he immediately regretted asking, wishing he could take it back.

"I'm sorry, please. It was an inappropriate question. I'm sorry, you—"

"It's alright," Catherine assured with a small sigh. "I didn't tell you much about him, did I?"

Simon shook his head and remained silent, still regretting his words.

"He was a good father and husband who died too soon. The doctor consulted other doctors, and no one could find out what plagued him." Catherine's voice was soft and serene. "He tried hard to make people think he was not suffering. Michelle and Stephen were young and didn't see his pain. For that, I am thankful. Their memories of him are good. They missed him a lot. We all did. As the years go by, we remember his death and his life, but memories fade, don't they?"

"Yes, they can." Simon reached out for her hand and saw color rise to her cheeks. Her hand was soft and warm. "But the heart does not forget either." Her eyes filled with compassion, and she offered a thankful smile.

"Thank you. Simon." The sound of his name on her lips was beautiful. "I appreciate your comfort."

He let go of her hand and turned to face the opposite direction. "As much as I could do this all day now, I think I should walk you back to the farmhouse."

"Oh, there's no need." Catherine looked at the view and back to him. "I made my way here. I can make my way back."

"I know." Simon held out his arm and raised a brow with a cheeky grin. "But I hope you won't mind if an old-fashioned man wants to escort his bride home, do you?"

She flushed at the word *bride,* and he thought it was adorable.

"No, I guess not." Catherine took his arm with a content smile; there was a soft glow in her eyes.

"I'm glad to be showing Stephen the ropes. He's quite interested in the neighbor's cattle, though," Simon remarked casually as they fell in step in the direction of the farmhouse. "Maybe you wouldn't mind him learning cattle driving and the like?"

"He's spoken of it, but he doesn't know how to ride a horse properly yet." Catherine's brows closed as concern filled her face.

"That's not a problem," Simon declared with a reassuring smile. "He'll get the hang of it. We all look out for each other, and you'll see, in time, how we help each other out."

Time went by quickly as they approached the farmhouse. As they stepped up from the back, the kitchen door burst open. Michelle and Stephen ran out as if a herd of buffalo was chasing after them. Their pale faces appeared horrified, and Simon felt his body stiffen. Catherine's hand disappeared from his arm, and she ran toward them, demanding to know what was wrong.

"There's… there's this lady inside," Stephen panted, "and she says…"

Without hearing another word, Simon barged inside his house. Who dared to come into his home uninvited and scare his children? He entered the living area, and he stopped dead in his tracks.

No, it couldn't be?

The woman noticed his presence and stood with a serene but uncomfortable smile. He saw the confused distress on Catherine's face.

"Harriet?" Simon croaked, and his chest thumped. He felt the wind had knocked the air out of every part of his body and heard gasps and whispers. "What are you doing here?"

"Hello, Simon." Harriet's voice was smooth, "It's good to see you." Her lips parted and unveiled a perfect smile.

CHAPTER FIVE

Catherine felt a rush of emotions as she saw Simon's ex-wife standing in the middle of the living room with a bright smile. Her dark brown hair hung loosely around her shoulders, and her skin seemed to shine. He had mentioned her in passing, how she had written him a letter and left, and how he had considered the marriage over. Still, Catherine had no idea how beautiful and young Harriet was. She glanced between them and was in no doubt that Harriet still loved him.

"Let's go. Stephen. Michelle, give them some space." Catherine whispered and hoped she appeared to be brave. But, right now, she felt anything other than brave.

Did Harriet want to get back with Simon? she wondered. Did that mean she would need to return to Lindsay Manor and beg for her employment back?

She knew they would not be able to stay in Carson anymore. It would be too painful.

She heard Simon call her name as she led the children out to the back. He sounded distressed, but she could not be in the room with them. Her heart pulled in different directions, and she thought she would burst.

"Is that lady right, Mom?" Stephen demanded, still shocked, when they were outside and out of earshot.

"Who is that woman?" Michelle blurted.

"Is that Mr. Perry's wife?"

Michelle stared at Stephen in horror. "How can that woman be his wife if he is to marry our mother?"

Catherine felt their eyes narrow in on her, and she bit her trembling lip. She had to be brave, she told herself, she had to be brave.

"Harriet is Simon's ex-wife," Catherine corrected and drew in a slow deep breath.

"Why is she here?" Staring at Michelle was like looking into a mirror and visioning a youthful reflection.

"I don't know, love," Catherine replied, trying to hide the rush of emotions that peaked at every question. "I don't think Simon was expecting her."

"Is there even something like an ex-wife?" Michelle asked and tried to pass around her mother to return inside, but Catherine stopped her.

"I've never heard of it," Stephen affirmed and exchanged a knowing glance with his sister.

"I don't understand. How are they married and not married?" Michelle insisted.

"Sit down, both of you." Catherine felt her emotional state transform into irritation. "Stop asking so many questions. Sit. I'll tell you everything."

Stephen and Michelle complied and chose empty seats at the outside table. Catherine watched the breeze rustle through their hair and noticed the color had slowly returned to their pale faces. Once they had seated, she wasted no time in answering their questions before they could come up with more.

"Simon was married before the war, and when he came back home, his wife, Harriet, or ex-wife now, had left him." Catherine paused as Michelle and Stephen's jaws slacked, and they stared at her, wide-eyed. Her mouth felt dry, and she licked her lips and continued. "She left a note for him in his office. This was when he still managed and lived at the grocery store."

"That's terrible," Michelle responded after a moment's silence. "Why did she do that?"

"I don't know. Maybe she stopped believing he would return home," Catherine answered with a small shrug.

"Does she think she can come back and push us out?" Stephen's voice heightened and gave way to a small croak.

"Stephen," Catherine scolded, "You shouldn't say that."

"What are you going to do, Mom?" Michelle's voice was calm, and her face clouded.

"I won't let that happen.," Stephen's eyes turned damp, and his lips pursed.

"Whatever happens, just remember that I love you both." Catherine huddled near them and pulled each one into a firm hug. "Simon has enjoyed you both very much, but I think we may just need to take matters into our own hands."

"What do you mean?" Michelle looked at her quizzically. "You don't mean... to leave?"

"If Simon decides to take Harriet back, then we cannot stay. I know how fond you are of him, but..." Her words trailed off at the thought of never seeing Simon again. Could she do it? Could she leave and think nothing of it? If so, why did her heart feel scorched?

"Why would he want her back?" Stephen sounded aghast. "She left him for dead."

"Stop it, Stephen." Catherine felt anger stir. "You cannot say that."

"Why not? It's true." He lifted his chin defiantly, and Catherine saw the hurt in his eyes.

"Let's be patient and wait for Simon." Catherine breathed in deeply. "You both stay here. I'll go inside and bring you something to drink."

"I don't trust her," Catherine heard Stephen say to Michelle as she entered the kitchen.

***

Catherine pinched her arm to check whether she was in a dream or nightmare, but no, it was real. The pinch hurt.

She gathered cups onto a tray and filled a pitcher with water. Although she did not hear voices from the living room, she tried hard to be as quiet as possible.

Simon had shared his moments of grief in the letters they exchanged, and she understood how Harriet's return would affect him. Maybe it would help if she and the children left. Then, Simon would not need to make a choice and feel guilty about someone being hurt. She did not want to put him in that position.

"Catherine?" Simon's appearance startled her. His husky voice held emotion, and he breathed out a sigh of relief. "I thought you had gone."

"Gone? No, we are outside. I'm taking a pitcher of water to the table." She felt her heart pound in her ears. "Will you and Harriet join us? I'll get more cups."

"Harriet? No, she's gone." He rubbed his temples with a thumb and forefinger.

"Gone? What happened?" Catherine mused.

"I'll tell you outside." He pushed her outside, and they found the table empty.

"Where are Stephen and Michelle?" Simon inquired and looked at her staring at two empty chairs where her children had been seated.

"I don't know. They were both upset." She placed the tray on the table and slumped in one of the empty chairs. Simon poured them both cups of water and sat beside her.

"I'm sorry." Simon offered her a cup, which she gratefully accepted. "Harriet is the last person I expected to ever see again, let alone come here. I don't know how she found out I bought a farm."

"What does she want?" Catherine saw beads of sweat had gathered along his brow, and he looked uncomfortable.

"It's been years," he said. He sounded distraught, and his voice warbled. "The last time I saw her, she was waving me goodbye. I didn't know at the time it was for good. Now, when I'm finally getting things together, and I feel happy… now she decides to seek me out. She wants me to take her back after all this time."

"I understand." Catherine tried a brave smile., "If it would make it easier, then Stephen, Michelle, and I can leave within the next few days."

His head whipped up and her breath caught in her throat at his intense gaze.

"You want to leave?" he asked quickly, and sadness filled his eyes.

"No, it was just a thought." Catherine placed the cup to her lips. "Maybe you and Harriet need space to talk over everything."

"What gives you that idea?" Simon spoke fast, and his tone became anxious. "I don't think there's anything left for either of us to say." His eyes locked onto hers, and Catherine was uncertain whether it was her heart or his she heard pounding in her ears.

"I should go look for Stephen and Michelle." Catherine looked away.

"No, it's best you stay in case they return to the house. I'll go look for them," Simon insisted. "They couldn't have gone far." She watched him down his water before heading toward the stables.

***

"Mom won't like this," Michelle whispered indignantly to her brother, who told her to shush with a flap of his hand.

After Catherine had left them outside, Stephen got up and walked around to clear his head. Within minutes, he raced back to Michelle and convinced her to follow him.

"I see her," Stephen said and arched his head forward. Michelle and Stephen had hidden behind a large rock formation. They had followed Harriet to the farm's boundary and watched her discretely enter a dilapidated shed that could have been used to store hay once.

"Why is she going in there?" Michelle frowned, "Didn't you say she was staying at an inn?"

"Yes, that is what she told Mr. Perry."

"This is a long way from the inn, and she has been inside for…" She noticed he was not listening. "Stephen, listen…"

"I'm going closer," Stephen whispered hoarsely behind him and ignored his sister's protests.

Michelle was not going to wait. If anything happened to him, she would never forgive herself. She felt shivers run down her spine as her skin brushed against the old, coarse wood.

"Wasn't Harriet alone?" Michelle inquired after hearing two voices from inside. She stared at her brother in horror.

Although the voice was muffled, she could hear Harriet talking to a man.

"No, he didn't listen to what I had to say. There was another woman there with children."

"You promised… he would … money… farm…" The male voice sounded angry.

"Stop, I told you." Harriet's smooth voice from earlier became agitated. "He will listen to me and take me back. Then we move forward with our plan."

"What?" Michelle blurted, and the voices inside stopped.

"Run, Michelle." Stephen's face was panic-stricken, and they ran, not paying attention to whether Harriet saw them or not.

CHAPTER SIX

Simon's steps were brisk as he took in the fresh, crisp air. After his conversation with Catherine, he needed to go for a walk and clear his head anyway. Save for the rustling of the wind, the stables were dead quiet. Where did those two mischievous children run off to now? They needed to come home now; the sun would start to set soon.

He felt a wash of emotion sweep over him at the memory of Catherine's expression, realizing who Harriet was. In a moment's weakness, he remembered everything he had felt for Harriet, but it did not take long to realize that it was past. He did not love her anymore. Harriet had not taken kindly to that and had stormed off a bit upset.

Tomorrow he would sit Catherine down and tell her everything that he and Harriet had spoken about. Still, for now, he had to get over the shock of seeing Harriet again. But first, he had to find Michelle and Stephen.

He decided to check the hay barn. Often, he caught Stephen trying to fool around with the haystacks. He would not be surprised if he found the barn messy with upturned bales of hay.

He neared the hay barn and heard a commotion. He quickened his pace and—*bam*, collided with them as he stepped foot inside.

"What's going on?" Simon almost toppled over. They were lying on their backs on the ground and seemed a bit out of breath.

"Where've you been, Mr. Perry?" Stephen said as he stood to his feet. "We've been looking everywhere for you."

"Me?" Simon raised a suspicious brow, and they both nodded. "I've been looking for you. Your mother is worried sick since you snuck away."

"I told you, Stephen," Michelle said angrily, and he observed she was ashen. "I knew Mom would be upset."

"But it was to help you," Stephen stammered and looked up at Simon.

"What are you talking about?" Simon felt annoyance creep over him. "Let's get back home; your mom wants to see you."

"But we followed that lady, Harriet," Stephen continued. "We know who she is, Mr. Perry, but she can't be trusted."

Simon frowned. "Trusted? Stop speaking in riddles. What's going on?"

"I followed Stephen to keep him out of trouble," Michelle offered. "There is this broken-down barn or shed hidden behind some trees before you come into your farm."

"You went all the way over there?" Simon stared at them incredulously. "That's a good mile away. I hope you didn't go inside. It isn't safe."

"It was safe for Harriet," Michelle replied. "And… for that other guy."

"What other guy?" Simon turned his head as if trying to hear them better. "It was just Harriet."

"No, there was a man inside," Stephen interjected vehemently, " and he wanted to take your money, your farm, and… something else."

"Mr. Perry, the man said Harriet should do all that." Michelle clarified, staring at him.

"We can show you," Stephen offered, but Simon held up his hand and motioned them to be quiet.

"I know which old barn you went to, and I'll check for myself. You both need to see your mom now," Simon elaborated sternly. The last thing he wanted was for them to follow him. "Can I count on you,

Michelle?" He received a firm nod. "You'll take your brother back to the house?"

"Yes, Mr. Perry. I'll make sure he comes with me." Michelle gave her brother a stern look.

Simon watched with a slight grin as a sheriff-like sister dragged away her gloomy-looking brother to their mother.

***

The old barn had not changed much since the last time Simon saw it. It was still old, dusty… and overall looked sad. He was surprised it was still holding out and made a mental note to speak to Barry Jenkins about tearing it down.

He dismounted his horse—there was no way he was going to walk all that way from home to the barn and back—and walked over to the front door and entered the barn. Not that he didn't believe them, but the children were right. There were handprints at the door and signs someone had been up here. Maybe two or three people.

Whether the marks were from outsiders or Stephen and Michelle, it was definitely not a place for children to play, and he did not want them returning either.

The ride back home seemed to take longer than riding out. Perhaps it was because the sun was setting and would be dark soon. He wondered whether it would be better to speak to Catherine tonight rather than in the morning, but he felt worn-out and tired.

He was relieved to arrive back home and found the table had been set early. Between Catherine and Michelle, they had worked hard for dinner. Michelle helped serve the roasted beef, and Stephen's face looked downcast.

"I had a look at that old barn, kids." Simon noticed their eager eyes as he took a bite of his meat and spooned his vegetables. "No one was there when I went there, but I don't want you going there again, alright?"

Catherine stopped eating. "Old barn?"

Both Michelle and Stephen agreed wistfully, and Simon quickly explained about the barn.

"I'll help the neighbor tear it down," Simon added and observed that Catherine's face looked troubled. He wondered if it had something to do with Harriet.

"I hope seeing Harriet today wasn't too much of a shock." Simon's brows knitted, and he noticed she flinched at the sound of Harriet's name.

"Carson was once her home." Catherine tried to smile, but he saw it had been hard for her. "I can't imagine what she must've thought or felt after seeing the farm."

"She was surprised. Never thought I'd be the farmer type. She's missed out, you know," Simon continued. "I expect she won't stay in Carson for much longer, though."

"Oh?" Catherine appeared stunned. "I thought she would stay."

"There is no reason for her to be here." Simon reached for another serving of coffee.

"I was thinking and talking everything over with Michelle and Stephen." Catherine drew in a deep breath. "Perhaps we should leave for a while…"

"No," Simon interrupted and shook his head. "Please don't leave because of Harriet. I don't want you to leave. You came out all this way. It's not fair to have you leave because she shows up at the doorstep."

"Alright." Catherine did not look convinced, but her lips curved into a small smile. "We'll stay right where we are."

CHAPTER SEVEN

Catherine walked into Michelle's room. Like her brother, her bag was left untouched, and she felt annoyed. Last night she had gone to great lengths explaining why they needed to leave.

Michelle and Stephen had promised they would pack their belongings at first light. Unfortunately, it was now late morning, and she could not find either of them.

What was she going to do? If she told Simon, he would try to convince her not to leave. She believed it would be the best for Simon and would help him decide what he truly needed to be happy. Catherine believed that she and her children were in the way, and she didn't want to be in the way of another's chance at happiness.

Catherine looked out the window at the cloudless dull blue sky. The wind took up leaves and scattered them in every direction.

John Smith's buggy was parked at the front, and to her surprise, Michelle was with him. She hurried downstairs and made her way outside as fast as she could.

"Michelle?" Catherine yelled out as soon as she had opened the front door, panting. "Where have you been? Where is your brother?"

"Good day, Mrs. Myers," John greeted politely, and she wanted the ground to swallow her up.

"I'm sorry, John. Hello. It's been quite a morning…" she started and saw him laughing with Michelle, who sat comfortably beside him, perched inside the buggy.

"Michelle?" Catherine pressed. "Where are you going? Isn't there something you need to do first?"

"Like what, Mom?" Michelle replied nonchalantly.

John turned a shade of beet. "Forgive me, Mrs. Myers. I had Michelle help with deliveries, and right now, I need her assistance. With your blessing, uh, approval, that is… I need her help, and it won't take long. Simon said it would be fine. The grocery store has been bustling this morning."

"I guess so," Catherine said slowly with a slight frown and gave Michelle a stern '*just wait until you get back, young lady*' look. The young girl pursed her lips and stared down at her feet.

"Thank you, Mrs. Myers. I think Stephen is with Simon in the fields," John added. He tugged at the reins, the horse began a slow trot, and the buggy lurched forward.

She waved them goodbye, brushing away wisps of hair that had escaped her low bun.

Catherine was about to go back inside the house, but she heard the sound of a rider approaching, and her eyes widened. It was Harriet riding on a chestnut American Quarterback. Why was she coming here?

She watched Harriet dismount and greeted her as she came closer.

"Hello, it's good to see you again," Harriet gushed with a sweet smile and walked up to Catherine, still standing on the porch.

Although she wore woman's riding attire, her hair had been taken up into a stylish chignon and was covered by a blue silk hat.

"Hello, Harriet," Catherine welcomed her with a smile. "Simon isn't here. He will be back soon… You can—"

"I'm not here to see Simon," Harriet interrupted politely, rendering Catherine speechless. "I came to see you."

"Oh? Well, I—I'll put on a kettle for coffee," Catherine managed, trying not to show her apprehension. She allowed Harriet to enter first. Why did Harriet want to see her?

While Harriet seated herself in the living room, Catherine brought out biscuits and placed them on the oak table.

"Can I help you with anything?" Catherine sat on a single couch and smoothed out her skirt.

"No, I'm just curious how you met Simon," Harriet said casually, taking Catherine by surprise. "You're not from around here, are you?" She leaned forward and searched the plate before plucking a biscuit.

"No. We moved here from Pennsylvania," Catherine answered hesitantly, wondering about Harriet's intent.

The familiarity that she adopted was as if they had known each other for years.

"You know, everybody in town knows about you," Harriet's voice carried through the air like a lullaby.

"I assume they would." Catherine followed suit and chose a biscuit. "The farm does supply the grocery store where we make regular supply trips."

"Of course. Yes, the farm." Harriet nodded thoughtfully and swallowed. The kettle whistled, and Catherine got up to make the coffee. Within a couple of minutes, she had reseated herself, and both she and Harriet nursed cups of coffee.

"Are you alright?" Catherine noted the other woman seemed a little anxious.

Harriet smiled calmly. "Yes, of course I am. Soon I will be with my true love again."

"That's good. I'm happy for you." Catherine felt confused as she recalled Simon's words when the subject came up over dinner, but thought better of saying anything.

"Did you think you were going to marry him?" Harriet asked suddenly, and Catherine almost choked on her coffee.

"Yes, I did. It was, after all, why my children and I moved to Simon's farm."

"Did he not say why I was here?" Harriet inquired and tasted the coffee.

"Yes, he did." Catherine was mystified as Harriet seemed unaware that Simon did not intend to reconcile with her. If so, it wouldn't be fair to expect Catherine to rectify that problem. "Has he spoken to you?"

Harriet sighed and placed her hands on her lap. "I only want to help you, you know. It may be best for you and your children to leave. Simon isn't the type to have more than one woman."

Flabbergasted, Catherine stood to her feet. Though leaving had been her plan, she did not like hearing the other woman mention it. "I'm about to prepare lunch and can set another table space for lunch if you want to join us. Afterward, you and Simon need to talk."

"No, Catherine, wait." Harriet grabbed her hand. "I think I have made myself clear. I am a better choice. I am younger, prettier, and I can bear Simon's children." Catherine stared at her as Harriet looked over her. "I suppose you could if you wanted to, but any more would ruin your figure."

"I am going to say this only once. Harriet, please leave and come back when Simon is here." Catherine could barely steady her voice as she was racked with anger and embarrassment. How dare Harriet say those things about her?

A booming voice took both women by surprise, suppressing Catherine's anger.

"Harriet. Do as she says and leave." Simon filled the doorframe, and Catherine shuddered at the intensity of his angry eyes. She felt her cheeks grow pink. Did he hear *all* Harriet had said?

"Oh, Simon…" Harriet's voice trembled, and her face paled. "I didn't… know… you were there."

Simon stepped inside and was replaced by Stephen's lanky frame. Stephen's face was pallid, and he rushed over to Catherine, who pulled him into a firm hug.

"How dare you speak unkindly about Catherine." Simon's voice dropped a pitch but still held fury mixed with sadness. "This is not you, Harriet. Since when did you change? The Harriet I once knew would never say such things. You said you were leaving today."

"But Simon, don't you think it's true?" Harriet's voice seemed to beg and plead with him.

"None of it is true," Simon bellowed and folded his arms, adding in a calmer tone. "Please leave now, Harriet. You've overstayed your welcome."

"Maybe she's right," Catherine said weakly as tears welled up. She was certain she could not be further humiliated.

"No, she's not," Simon sounded surprised.

"Don't you want a boy of your own?" Catherine asked and felt hot liquid fall down her cheeks.

"I will have one, soon," Simon affirmed softly and looked at Stephen with fondness. "There he is."

"I mean…" Catherine paused and tried to steady her shaky voice. "Don't you want a son of your own blood?"

"That's right, Simon." Harriet took the opportunity. "We spoke of having our son many times…"

"Quiet, Harriet," Simon ordered, his eyes never leaving Catherine. "It's time you take your exit." Simon placed his finger underneath Catherine's chin and lifted her face until their eyes locked. "I've not changed my mind. I love you, Catherine Myers."

"No, Simon." Harriet burst into tears. "You don't mean that, you don't. I know you don't."

Catherine felt her heart pound harder, and her stomach felt like it had twisted into knots many times over.

"Simon, I—I…" Catherine sniffled, and her voice trailed off as a commotion was heard from the front door. Catherine heard John and Michelle's voices and a third voice she did not recognize. A male voice.

Stephen tugged on his mother's arm and gained both her and Simon's attention. "This is the man from the barn."

"Harriet." The gruff voice resonated throughout the house, and her face turned ghostly. "I'm sick of waiting. How much longer will this take? Harriet."

"What's the meaning of this?" Simon demanded, looking at Harriet. She appeared panic-stricken, and the male voice came closer.

"Luke Grant?" Simon's eyes widened, and he looked appalled. "Harriet, you left me for the likes of Luke?"

"I'm sorry, Simon. I didn't mean for all this," Harriet bawled, head buried in her hands, and collapsed onto the couch.

"Who's Luke?" Stephen whispered.

"My outlaw cousin," Simon replied, infuriated. "You bring him inside my house, too, Harriet?"

Luke appeared at the doorframe, boasting a golden tooth, and spoke with a defined drawl. "Hey, cuz, it's been a while, hey?"

"Get out of my house." Simon stepped toward him, hands clenched. "No one gave you permission to enter my house."

"Oh, yeah?" He jerked his head toward the door. "The girl outside looks like this woman here, and the guy she's with said I could. Gave 'em no choice, though. My gun's right here." He tapped his belt.

"Did you think you could steal from me, Luke?" Simon's voice was steady and challenging. "You have a lot of nerve coming into my home. State your business with Harriet."

"We had an agreement." Luke's grin was ominous, and Catherine felt the hair at the back of her neck rise. He was nothing like Simon. His dark hair was neat but had a greasy shine and partly covered eyes that were cold and dark.

"So you find out about my farm." Simon nodded thoughtfully. "And decide you can come take it from me? How did you expect to do that now, I wonder?"

"Plans have changed now that Harriet can't convince you to take her back." Luke sniggered and glanced over at her. "I don't need her anymore." He reached for his belt, and Simon stopped him.

"I wouldn't do that if I were you." Simon stared at him with an arched brow, pushed his shoulders back, and lifted his chin.

"You challenging me to a dual?" Luke's eyes narrowed, and he tilted his head. "Didn't think you were that stupid. Remember the time I almost broke your jaw?"

"Huh, we were kids," Simon scorned.

"Yeah? Well, then, you may as well be handing over your farm to me now," Luke said mockingly. "Where's your gun, cuz? I have a spare."

"Don't you worry about me. After you, *cousin*," Simon insisted. His smile was not friendly, and his eyes never left Luke as he stepped back.

Harriet chimed in, "Luke, no. You promised no one would get hurt."

"Didn't keep to your end of the bargain, did you?" Luke responded casually as he sauntered outside. Simon was close at his heels.

"You're not going through with this, are you?" Catherine followed him, as did the others. She could not believe what was happening. From being just about Harriet, it was now a conspiracy between Harriet and Luke to get money off Simon.

Michelle was crouching at the far end of the porch and ran over the moment she saw Catherine, tears streaming down her cheeks. "Mom, I'm sorry I left before. That man's dangerous. John knows him and has gone to call the sheriff."

"It's alright," Catherine hugged her tight. "Good on John."

Simon stopped at the porch and leaned in closer, so only Michelle and Catherine heard him whisper. "Don't worry. I know what I'm doing. I knew John would go get the sheriff."

"What's he doing?" Michelle asked as Catherine watched him walk down the porch steps and meet Luke standing at the bottom.

"I don't know." Catherine shook her head slowly. "I don't know what's going through his mind. They're having a duel. It seems Luke has a spare gun."

Catherine ignored the astounded look on Michelle's face and watched as the two men agreed to the nature of the duel.

She felt beads of perspiration gather at her temples at the sight of the two men standing back to back. What was Simon thinking? What was taking John and the sheriff so long?

While Luke held his gun in position, Simon pocketed the one Luke had given to him. Catherine frowned, and her heart beat faster the closer Luke got to the countdown. Then, as the men were about to march forward in the opposite directions, Simon pushed his foot behind him, twisted it, and caught Luke's ankle in midair, sending him sprawling headfirst to the ground and knocking him out.

"Looks like the duel is off," Simon remarked with a satisfied grin. "Stephen, go get me some rope." He walked behind Luke, nudged his knee dead center on his back, and pinned Luke's arms.

Stephen returned with the rope within minutes, and while Simon tied him up, John and the sheriff arrived.

Catherine was relieved when the sheriff left with Luke in tow, still passed out.

Harriet told her side of the story through tears. She admitted to bringing Luke to town but had no idea what he'd planned to do. She was recently widowed to Kyle Brand, who had passed away from a heart attack, and he had taken a loan from his brother. She needed money to pay it off, and Luke had agreed to help.

She left the farm soon after her confession and didn't want to stay for lunch.

Catherine had laid platters of fruit, salted beef, lemonade, and strong coffee outside and everyone gathered for a light lunch.

"Catherine, I want to ask you something," Simon said softly, and everyone stopped talking. "Do you really want to leave?"

She felt her face grow hot and shook her head. "No, I only wanted you to be happy, and I thought you loved Harriet."

"A part of me always will, I suppose, but that's the past." Simon stood to his feet and walked over to her. "There's a new chapter coming to my life soon, and I'm looking forward to that."

"You are?" She glanced at him with a soft smile.

"I know you were worried when Harriet came. None of us could have known that Luke was around, but that's all gone now." He crouched to his knees and took her hand. "Catherine, I love you, and I still would very much like to make you my bride if you will have me." His eyes glimmered, and Catherine felt her knotted stomach twist again.

"Yes, Simon Perry," she laughed pleasantly. "I would love to be your bride."

He stood upright, pulled her up, and planted a passionate kiss on her beautiful cherry lips.

EPILOGUE

Five years later

The farmhouse was in utter excitement as everyone prepared for the upcoming celebrations. Catherine was in Michelle's room, plaiting and tying up her hair. She looked at her daughter, standing tall, graceful, and beautiful, dressed in a stunning white wedding gown trimmed with lace and matching shoes. She was like a swan ready to take flight.

Thankfully, Laurie Smith had offered her services to help prepare the feast, enabling Catherine to focus most of her attention on Michelle.

"I love this dress, Mom." Michelle's smile was bright, and Catherine fought back tears. "I can't believe I'll soon be a married woman."

"Yes, my love." Catherine gave her daughter's shoulder a slight squeeze. "You and me both. I'm almost finished with your hair."

"Thank you, Mom. I feel so happy. I didn't know it was possible to feel this way." Michelle's voice caught in her throat.

"That is how you should be feeling, love," Catherine responded with a soft chuckle.

There was a knock at the door, and Simon entered with a giant smile. "How is the bride-to-be?" he asked. Then, when he saw Michelle, he added, "John is lucky to have you as his bride."

Michelle blushed and gave a small smile. "Thank you, Dad."

Catherine felt blessed to be with such a man who had been the best father he could be to Michelle and Stephen.

"Your brother is helping to hitch up the buggies for the trip to the church. I best go…"

"Dad…" Michelle cleared her throat. "I did some thinking, and I spoke to Mom." She paused and drew in a deep breath. "Everyone knows Mom and I had our own plans, but I would really like it if you could be the one to take me down the aisle."

Simon stared at her agape. He was speechless.

"Would you, Dad?" Michelle urged. "Please say you will."

"Of course, honey." Simon placed his hands on her shoulders and bore a large smile. "It would be my honor to take you down the church aisle."

She clapped her hands together and gave him a tender hug. "Thank you, Dad."

Catherine wiped her eyes. She did not realize tears had formed and were rolling down her cheek.

A couple of years ago, she would never have believed they could be as happy as they were now. She did not think that love could be felt twice. But she had been proven wrong. Simon proved that she could experience love again and happiness not just in her life but also in her children's lives.

"C'mon, Catherine," Simon called. He and Michelle were standing at the door.

She had been lost in her thoughts, and she had not noticed Michelle and Simon start to make their way downstairs.

"Go on. I'll join you in a minute." Catherine felt her face flush.

"Okay, don't take too long," Simon said with an affirmative nod, still beaming with pride.

She watched them leave the room in enthusiastic conversation, and the sight made her happy. She looked in the mirror and then hurried to join the others outside.

Stephen and the others had finished hitching the horses to the buggies. They were all in idle conversation until they saw Simon and Michelle appear.

Stephen's face looked astonished when he saw his sister.

"Are you my sister?" Stephen pushed out a mischievous smile and then added. "You look great, Michelle."

He was almost Simon's height, and his frame was beginning to bulk.

Michelle looked radiant. She leaned forward, kissed him on the cheek, and thanked him. Stephen's cheeks turned a deep crimson.

Catherine watched them tease each other and realized that the next time her daughter returned, it would be as a married woman. John was a good man, and she could only hope they would share many happy years together and experience the same love and happiness that would last a lifetime.

__The End__

Just to say thanks for checking our works we like to gift you

Our Exclusive Never Before Released Books

100% FREE!

Please GO TO

`http://cleanromancepublishing.com/gift`

And get your FREE gift

Thanks for being such a wonderful client.

Please Check out My Other Works

By checking out the link below

http://cleanromancepublishing.com/fjauth

Thank You

Many thanks for taking the time to buy and read through this book.

It means lots to be supported by SPECIAL readers like YOU.

Hope you enjoyed the book; please support my writing by leaving an honest review to assist other readers.

.

With Regards,

Faith Johnson

Printed in Great Britain
by Amazon

39181010R00078